D0969758

WHISPERS
from the
UNICORN

A journal which will bring the magic alive

BY FELICIA
STARSHINE

COPYRIGHTED MATERIAL

Copyright © 2018 Felicia Starshine

All rights reserved.

ISBN-13: 978-1986350204

ISBN-10: 1986350207

ACKNOWLEDGMENTS

Sincere gratitude to:

Edward Andes, for his invaluable contribution in making this journal a unique unicorn lover item

George Ndwiga, for his never-ending resourcefulness and excellent ideas

Harriet Warren, for being the abundant creative fountain she inherently is.

"Those who don't believe in magic will never find it. Those who don't believe in unicorns will never see one."

NAME YOUR UNICORN

WHERE DOES YOUR UNICORN LIVE?

WHAT DOES YOUR UNICORN DO FOR FUN?

Color in the unicorn below

Fill in the blank spaces

Once upon a time in a far, far away land where only unicorns existed, there was a lonely unicorn named.................. Nobody liked this unicorn because she had no wings to fly. Day and night she would cry tears filled with pink and blue glitter and she would long to find a best friend to play with.

On one of the sunniest days of the year where rainbows took over the sky and everyone danced and sang with happiness in their heart, the lonely unicorn decided to visit planet earth to find a friend, a friend who would teach her how to fly without wings and who could dance beside her.

She set off on her journey to an unknown world and that was where she came across the sleeping girl named............, with beautiful ....
eyes and it was there she knew she had found her home.

WHAT IS YOUR UNICORN NAME?

Combine the first letter of your name
With the month you were born in:

A	PERKY	N	CRAZY	JAN	TWINKLE TOES
B	BUBBLES	O	AWESOME	FEB	SUGAR SOCKS
C	PHOENIX	P	STARLIGHT	MAR	DAINTY EYES
D	SHINY	Q	SILLY	APR	HAPPY FEET
E	SPARKLES	R	RAINBOW	MAY	SNOWY HOOVES
F	SUNSHINE	S	MAGNIFICENT	JUN	FLOATING BUBBLES
G	CHIPPER	T	PRINCESS	JUL	SUMMER DREAM
H	TWINKLE	U	GIDDY	AUG	BLUE BERRY
I	SUNNY	V	LOVELY	SEP	SILVER MOON
J	JOLLY	W	DANDELION	OCT	GOLDEN TAIL
K	COLORFUL	X	FANCY	NOV	GLITTER LOVE
L	HAPPY	Y	BUTTERCUP	DEC	CANDY REINS
M	DAYDREAM	Z	SASSY		

FIND THE WORDS

```
L G X D P M M W
A L B Z G A O U
C I N P G B N S
I T R I N I M S
H T C I C A T D
T E A O E A P W
Y R R R R R D T
M N D S V Y X T
```

UNICORN
MYTHICAL RAINBOW
STARS
MAGIC   DREAMS
GLITTER

Embrace your uniqueness,
Stay true to you,

Believe in miracles,
Sparkle from within.

The little girl woke up with a startle, shocked and surprised to see a unicorn in her bedroom. "What, who, how did you get here?" she stammered.
"Please, I am only looking for a friend" whispered the unicorn with tears in her eyes.
"I would love to be your friend but how am I going to look after you, where will you sleep?"
"Here, I can hide and at night you can teach me to fly and dance, like all the other unicorns" said the unicorn with a smile.
The little girl laughed out loud and agreed, sure she was dreaming but when she touched the unicorns horn, silky and shiny and cool to touch, she knew this was real.

"OK, you can hide in here and when I get back from school, we will see what we can do. Don't leave this room and don't let anyone see you" the girl instructed.
She grabbed her clothes and headed out the door with one last glance at this magical creature sitting on her bed.

WHAT LAND DOES YOUR UNICORN COME FROM?

The
Pure Forest

The
Trance Region

The
Hidden Moon

The
Ember Isles

The
Autumn Realms

HOW TO DRAW A UNICORN

FOLLOW YOUR DREAMS

IF YOU WERE A UNICORN...

What would be your secret superpower?

• •

What color would your horn be?

• •

What color glitter would your house be made from?

• •

CONNECT THE DOTS

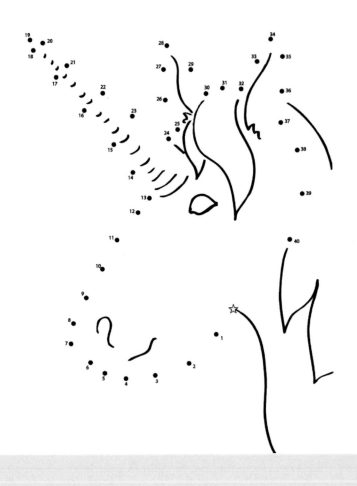

The little girl came home from school that day and saw the lonely unicorn crying more tears of glitter. "Why, don't cry, unicorn, I will help you."

The unicorn stood up and shook all the glitter off and said, "I know, I'm crying because I am sad but I am happy I found you."

"Well, let's go and have some fun" said the girl with a smile.

Off they went into the night and although the unicorn was different there were so many things they had in common. The little girl took the unicorn to the beach to see the sea, they rode together along the sand and ate ice cream on their way back. They spent every evening listening to music and dancing until they had no energy left.

Days passed until one evening the little girl said to the unicorn, "I can't teach you how to fly but you know, not everyone needs to be the same to fit in."

The unicorn stared at the girl and asked, "But all the other unicorns have wings, why don't I?"

"Well, you were born to be special. You see, I am terrible at math but I am the fastest runner in school. I hate art but I am really good at music."

The unicorn took a moment to think and said, "Are you sure because I can't fly and without wings I never will be able to"

The little girl stood up and opened up her wardrobe, she took out a pair of fairy wings she used for a fancy dress party and proudly presented them to the unicorn.

NAME ALL THE CONTINENTS YOU WANT TO VISIT WITH YOUR UNICORN

NAME ALL THE PLACES YOU HAVE BEEN TO

"You don't need wings but here are mine. Maybe they might help you find your own."

The unicorn began to cry and said to the little girl, "One day, someday I will be back. You have given me more than ice cream and cake, you have given me hope. I am going to see my family but I will return and give you back these wings because you never know, maybe one day you might need them too."

The little girl stood at her window and waved the unicorn goodbye and although she was sad she had left, she knew today was a good day, a really good day because she had helped the unicorn realize she didn't need wings to fly.

LESSONS FROM A UNICORN

There's magic inside you,
Anything is possible.
Dreams can come true,
You don't need wings to fly.

It's okay to be different. And always believe in
yourself even if nobody else does.

MY OPINION ABOUT UNICORNS

I think unicorns are..

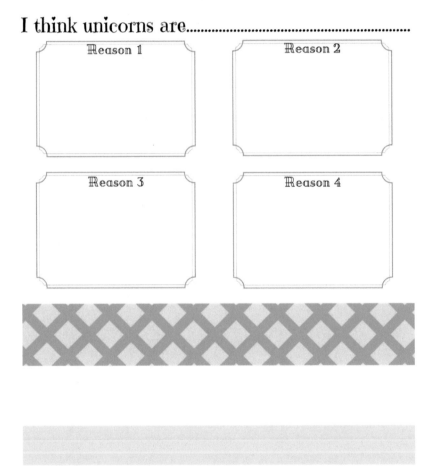

Reason 1

Reason 2

Reason 3

Reason 4

NAME YOUR TOP 4 UNICORN NAMES

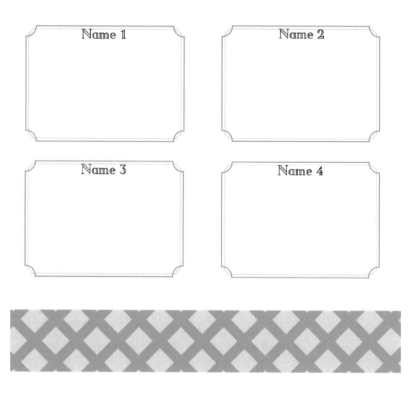

Name 1

Name 2

Name 3

Name 4

UNICORN CODE

1. Unicorns never cheat.
2. Unicorns always lend a helping hand.
3. Unicorns don't talk to strangers.
4. Unicorns respect the earth.
5. Unicorns are never late.
6. Unicorns don't judge people.
7. Unicorns always give 100%.
8. Unicorns graze on peace and love.
9. Unicorns don't do drugs.
10. Unicorns make the world a better place with kindness.

COLOR IN THE UNICORNS

SPOT THE DIFFERENCES

SURREAL

Lavender rainbows in teal green
skies
Where all clouds are lined silver
Glittered lakes in powder pink
Feed pastel unicorns with pearlesque
horns
Twisted in iridescent beauty
In a land of pretty pegasi
Dreams become reality

ABOUT THE AUTHOR

Felicia Starshine was born in a land far, far away where rainbows never ended, where rainstorms came down as glitter, where the mountains were soft like cotton wool and where everything was painted in color. Felicia was born among unicorns and even now until this day, she visits her much loved friends and sometimes even takes a ride to the moon with them.

Felicia learnt to treasure the good things in life and cherish the small moments which made her happy. By writing this journal for others to enjoy, she feels she is giving back just a little piece of magic, just as the unicorns gave to her.

THE END

42153004R00022

Made in the USA
Middletown, DE
11 April 2019